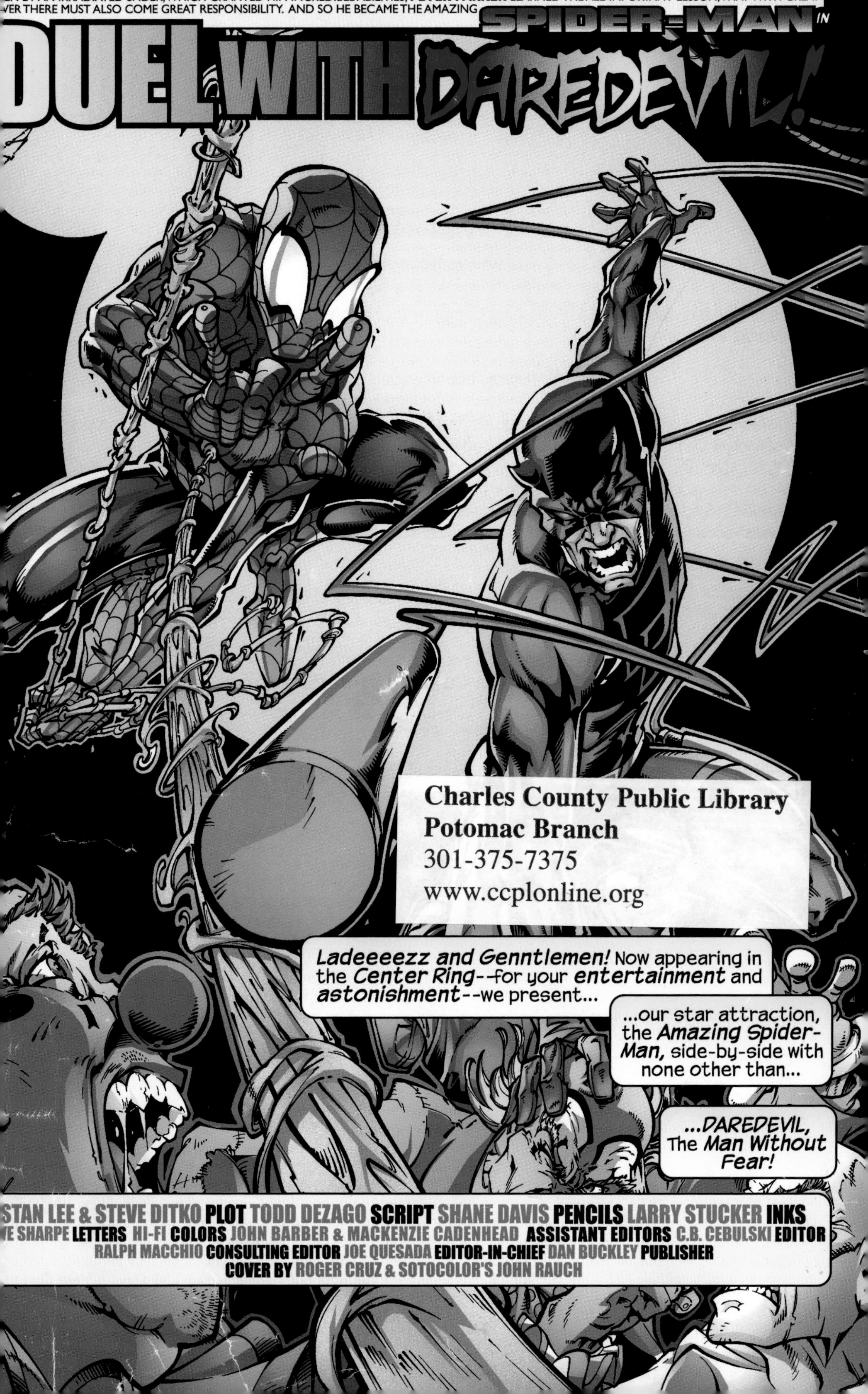

EN BY AN IRRADIATED SPIDER, WHICH GRANTED HIM INCREDIBLE ABILITIES, PETER PARKER LEARNED THE ALL-IMPORTANT LESSON, THAT WITH GREAT
VER THERE MUST ALSO COME GREAT RESPONSIBILITY. AND SO HE BECAME THE AMAZING SPIDER-MAN IN
DUEL WITH DAREDEVIL!
Ladeeeezz and Genntlemen! Now appearing in the Center Ring--for your entertainment and astonishment--we present...
...our star attraction, the Amazing Spider-Man, side-by-side with none other than...
...DAREDEVIL, The Man Without Fear!
STAN LEE & STEVE DITKO PLOT TODD DEZAGO SCRIPT SHANE DAVIS PENCILS LARRY STUCKER INKS
E SHARPE LETTERS HI-FI COLORS JOHN BARBER & MACKENZIE CADENHEAD ASSISTANT EDITORS C.B. CEBULSKI EDITOR
RALPH MACCHIO CONSULTING EDITOR JOE QUESADA EDITOR-IN-CHIEF DAN BUCKLEY PUBLISHER
COVER BY ROGER CRUZ & SOTOCOLOR'S JOHN RAUCH

VISIT US AT

www.abdopub.com

Spotlight, a division of ABDO Publishing Company Inc., is the school and library distributor of the Marvel Entertainment books.

Library bound edition © 2006

MARVEL, and all related character names and the distinctive likenesses thereof are trademarks of Marvel Characters, Inc., and is/are used with permission. Copyright © 2005 Marvel Characters, Inc. All rights reserved. www.marvel.com

MARVEL, Spider-Man: TM & © 2005 Marvel Characters, Inc. All rights reserved. www.marvel.com. This book is produced under license from Marvel Characters, Inc.

Library of Congress Cataloging-in-Publication Data

Duel With Daredevil!

ISBN 1-59961-013-2   (Reinforced Library Bound Edition)

All Spotlight books are reinforced library binding and manufactured in the United States of America

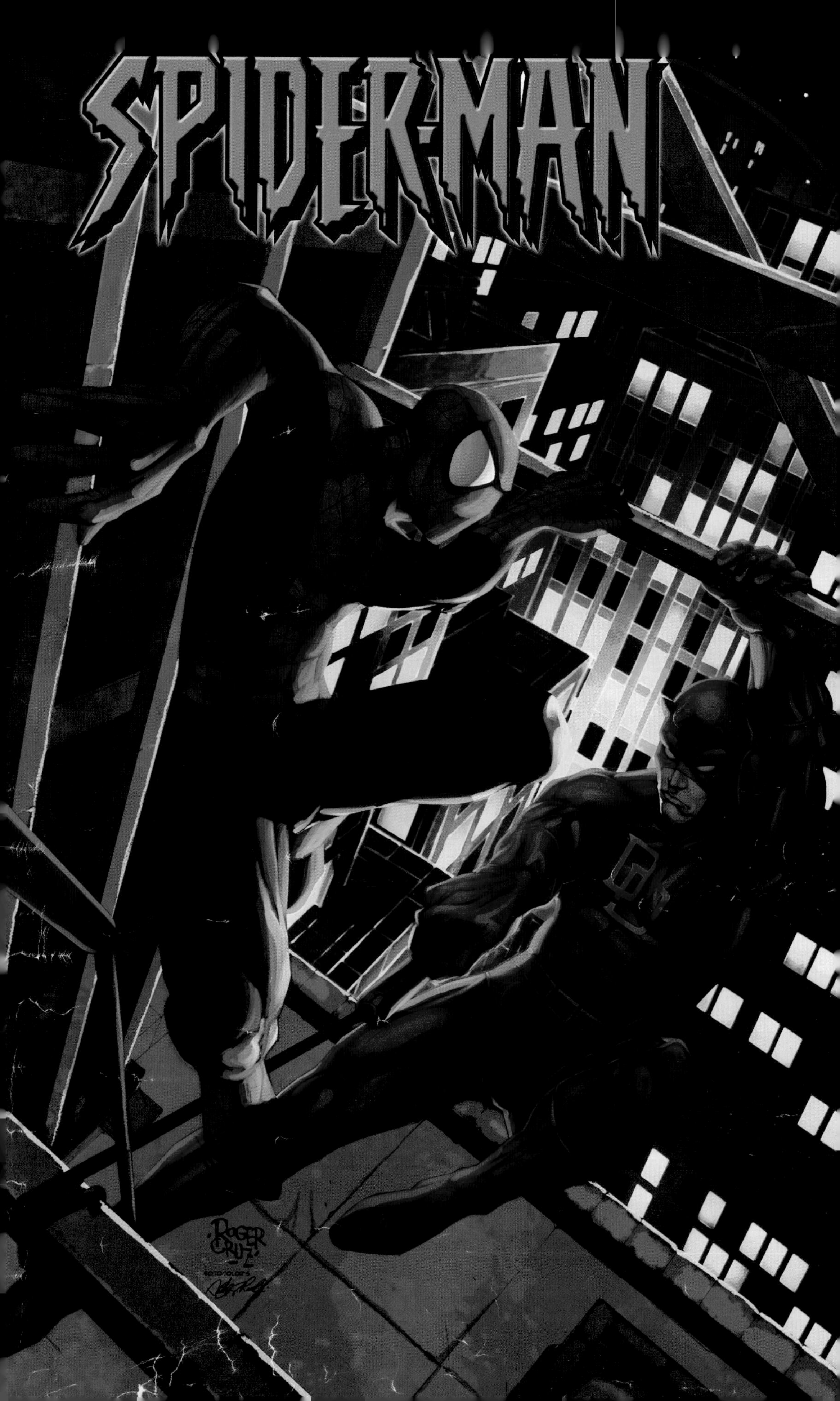
SPIDER-MAN
ROGER CRUZ

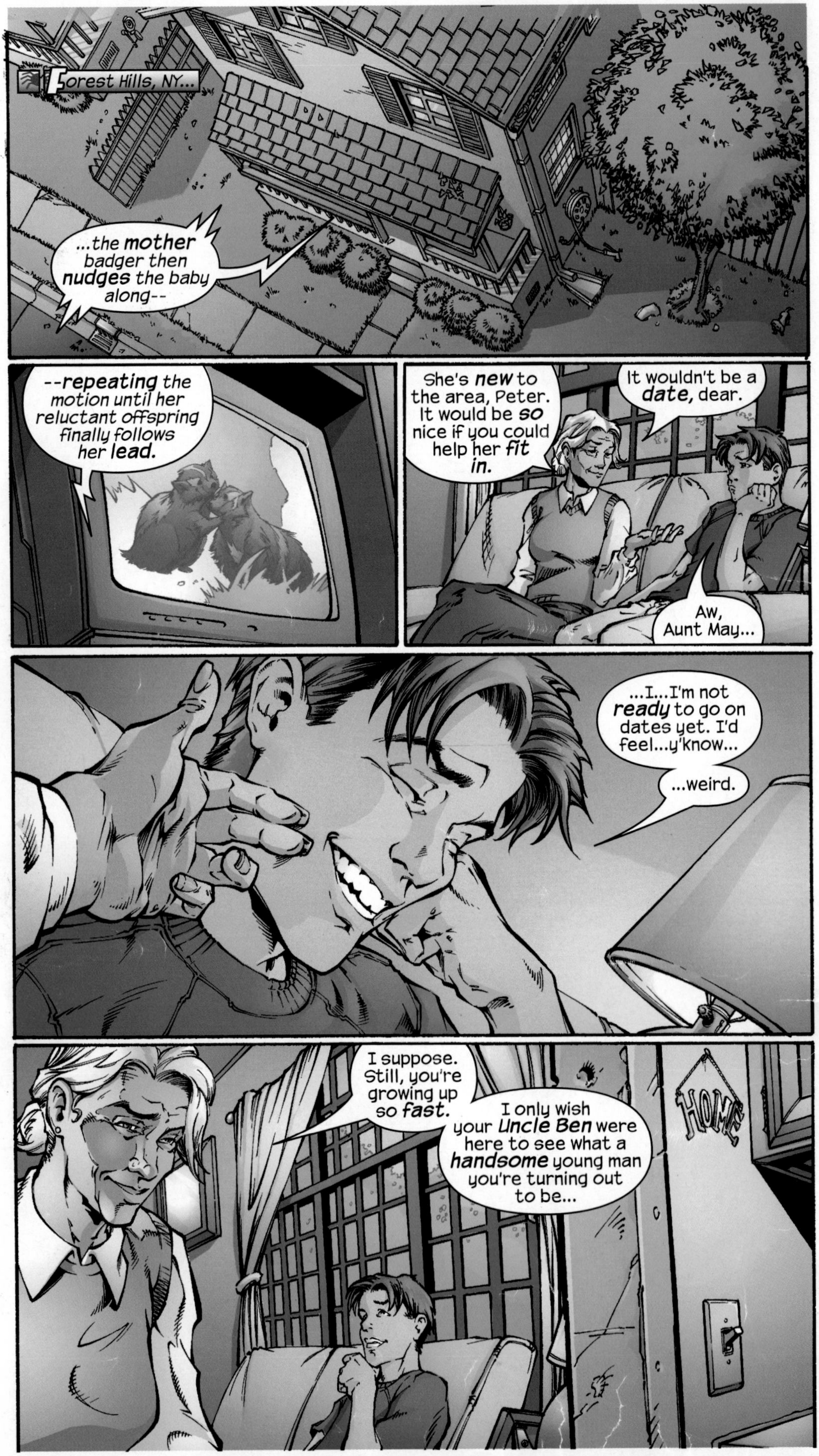

Forest Hills, NY...
...the mother badger then nudges the baby along--
--repeating the motion until her reluctant offspring finally follows her lead.
She's new to the area, Peter. It would be so nice if you could help her fit in.
It wouldn't be a date, dear.
Aw, Aunt May...
...I...I'm not ready to go on dates yet. I'd feel...y'know...
...weird.
I suppose. Still, you're growing up so fast.
I only wish your Uncle Ben were here to see what a handsome young man you're turning out to be...
HOME

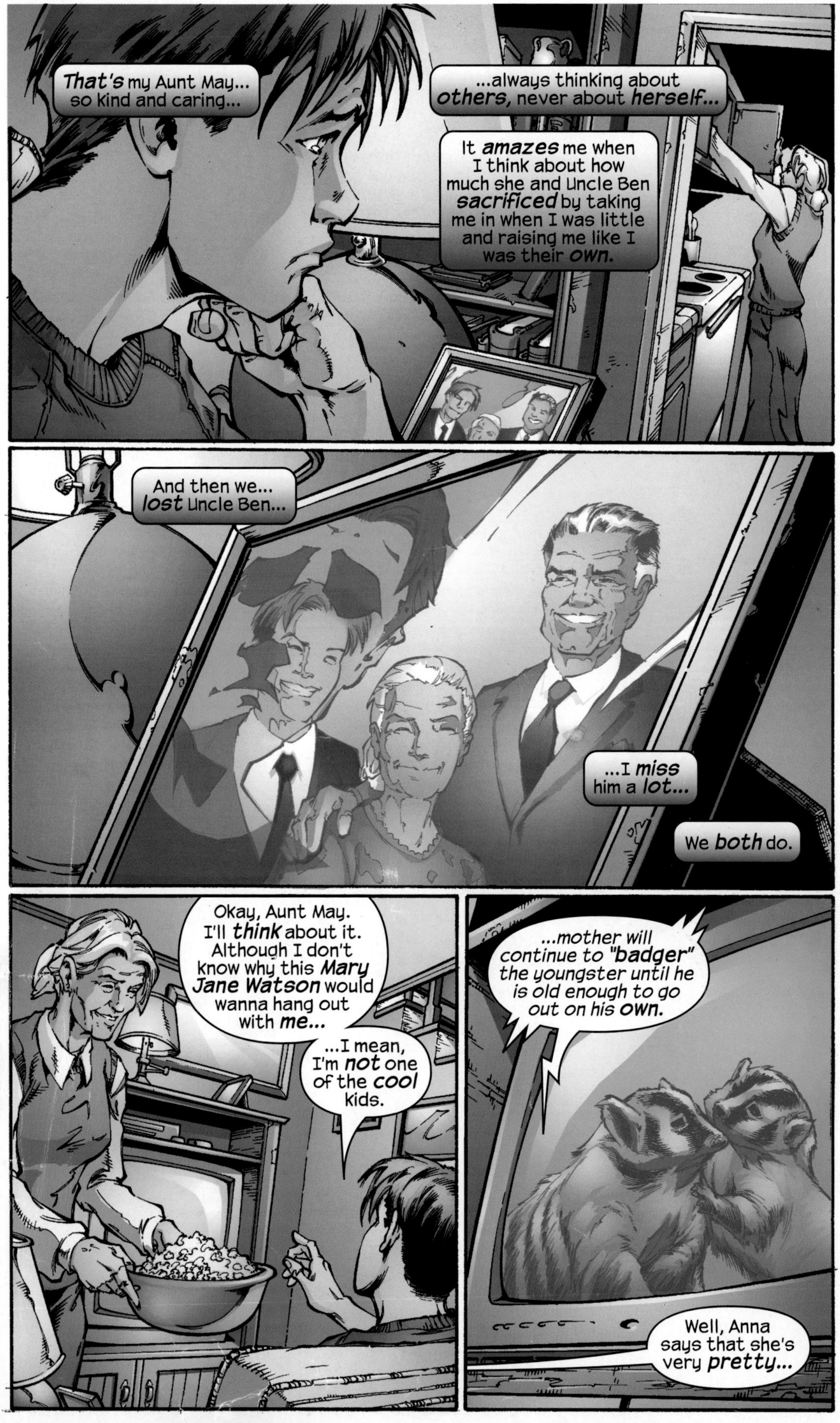
That's my Aunt May... so kind and caring...
...always thinking about others, never about herself...
It amazes me when I think about how much she and Uncle Ben sacrificed by taking me in when I was little and raising me like I was their own.
And then we... lost Uncle Ben...
...I miss him a lot...
We both do.
Okay, Aunt May. I'll think about it. Although I don't know why this Mary Jane Watson would wanna hang out with me...
...I mean, I'm not one of the cool kids.
...mother will continue to "badger" the youngster until he is old enough to go out on his own.
Well, Anna says that she's very pretty...

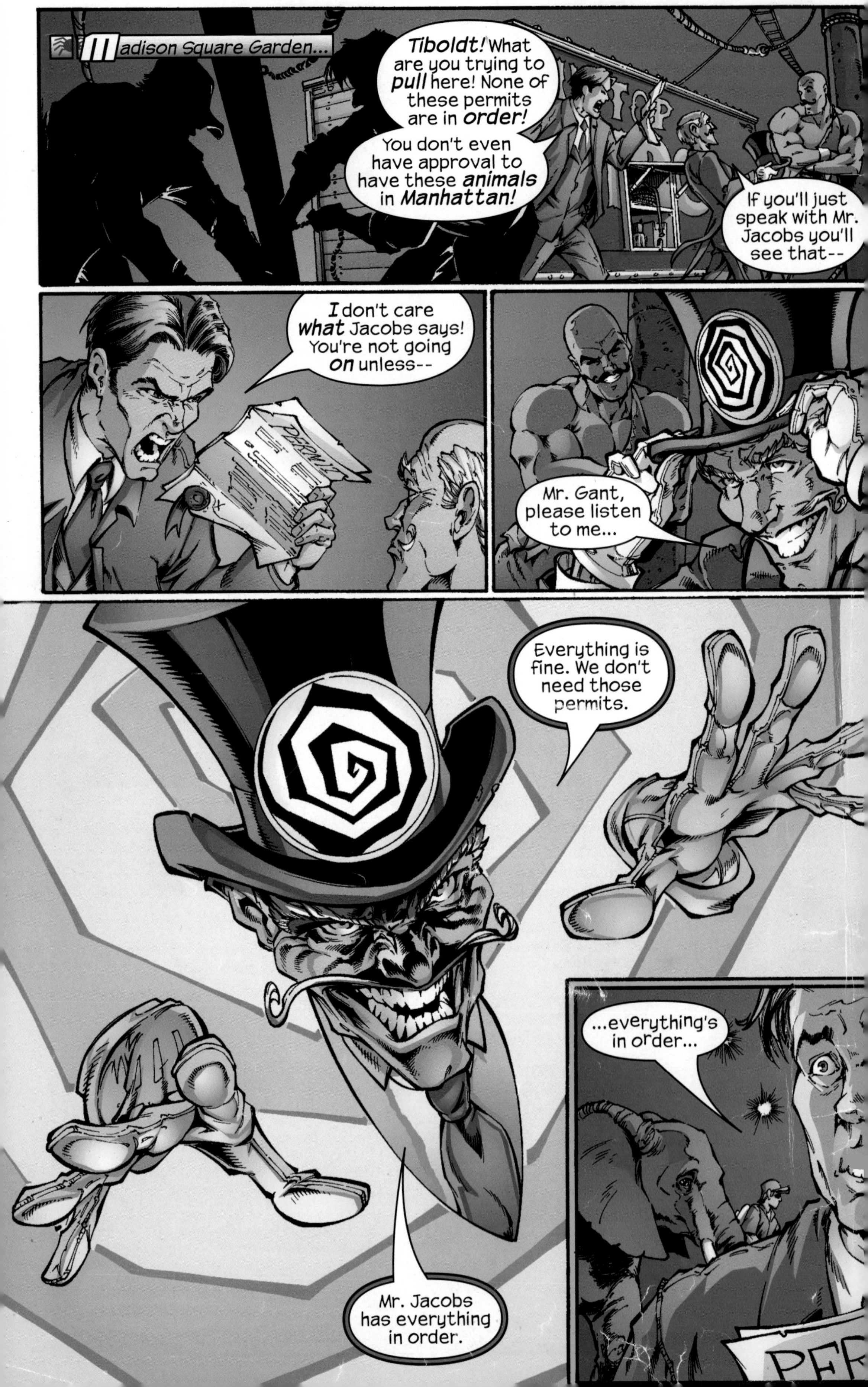
Madison Square Garden...
Tiboldt! What are you trying to pull here! None of these permits are in order!
You don't even have approval to have these animals in Manhattan!
If you'll just speak with Mr. Jacobs you'll see that--
I don't care what Jacobs says! You're not going on unless--
Mr. Gant, please listen to me...
Everything is fine. We don't need those permits.
Mr. Jacobs has everything in order.
...everything's in order...

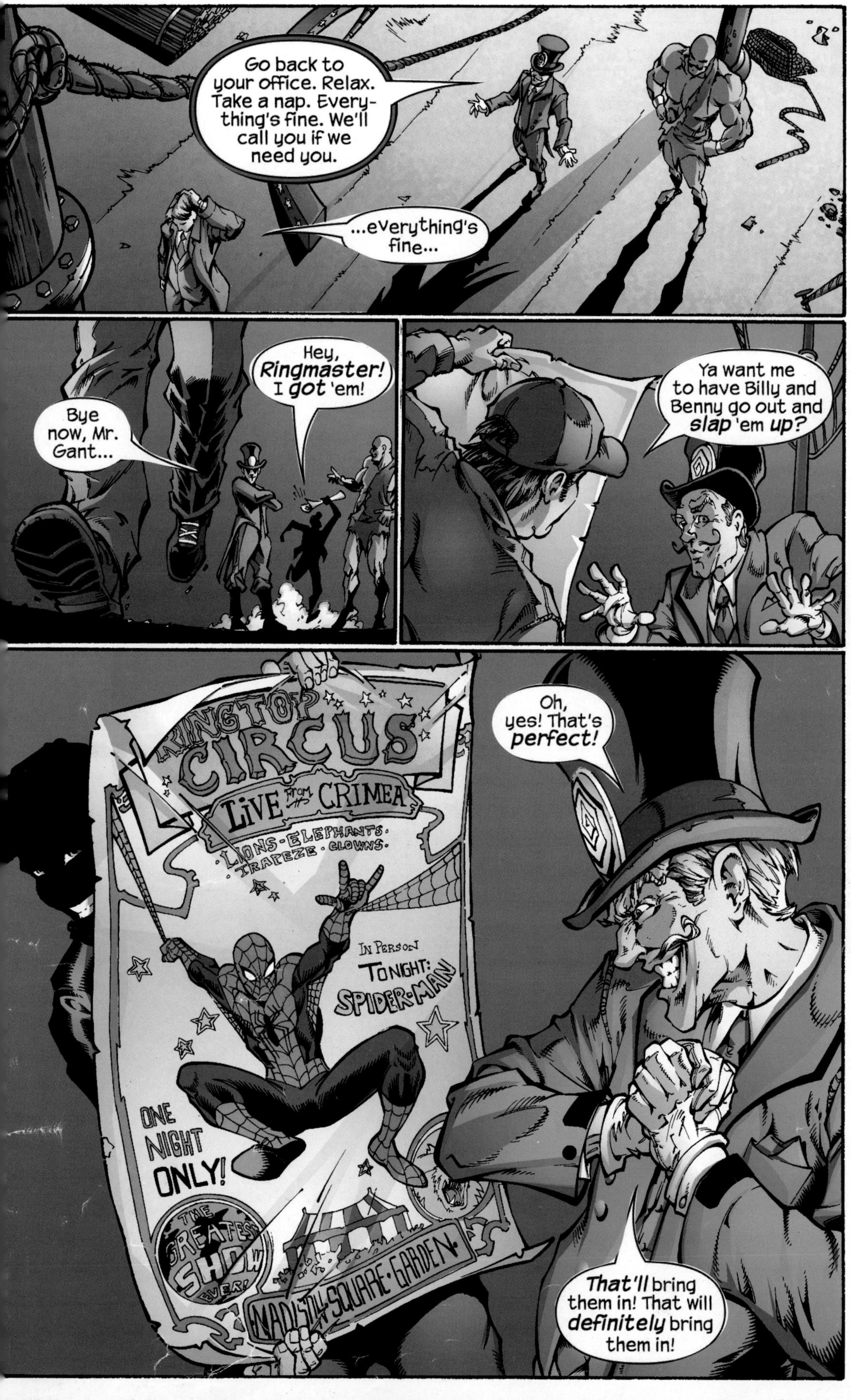

Go back to your office. Relax. Take a nap. Everything's fine. We'll call you if we need you.
...everything's fine...
Bye now, Mr. Gant...
Hey, *Ringmaster!* I *got* 'em!
Ya want me to have Billy and Benny go out and *slap* 'em *up?*
RINGTOP CIRCUS
LIVE CRIMEA
LIONS · ELEPHANTS · TRAPEZE · CLOWNS
IN PERSON
TONIGHT: SPIDER-MAN
ONE NIGHT ONLY!
THE GREATEST SHOW EVER!
SQUARE · GARDEN
Oh, yes! That's *perfect!*
That'll bring them in! That will *definitely* bring them in!

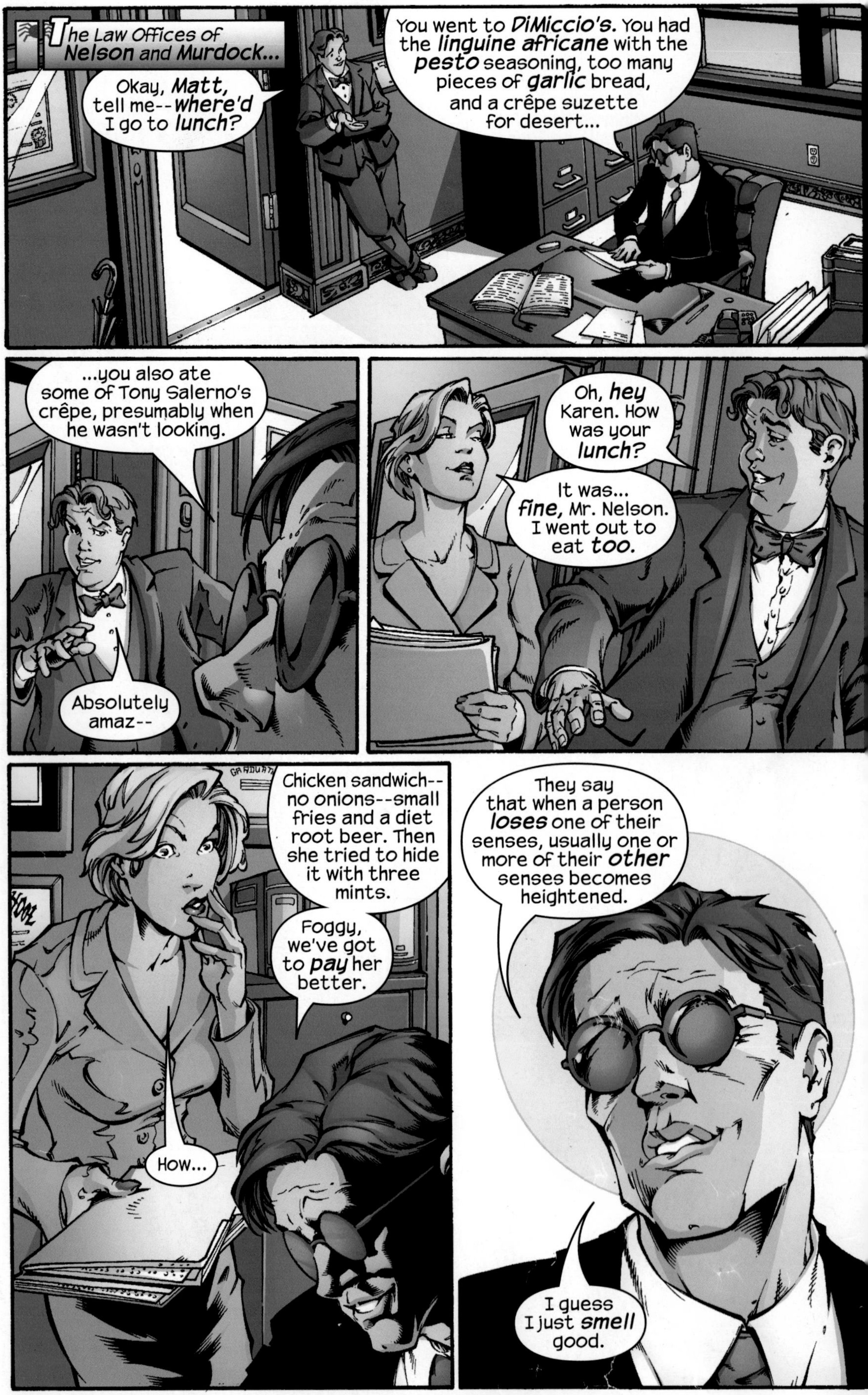
The Law Offices of Nelson and Murdock...
Okay, Matt, tell me--where'd I go to lunch?
You went to DiMiccio's. You had the linguine africane with the pesto seasoning, too many pieces of garlic bread, and a crêpe suzette for desert...
...you also ate some of Tony Salerno's crêpe, presumably when he wasn't looking.
Absolutely amaz--
Oh, hey Karen. How was your lunch?
It was... fine, Mr. Nelson. I went out to eat too.
Chicken sandwich--no onions--small fries and a diet root beer. Then she tried to hide it with three mints.
Foggy, we've got to pay her better.
How...
They say that when a person loses one of their senses, usually one or more of their other senses becomes heightened.
I guess I just smell good.

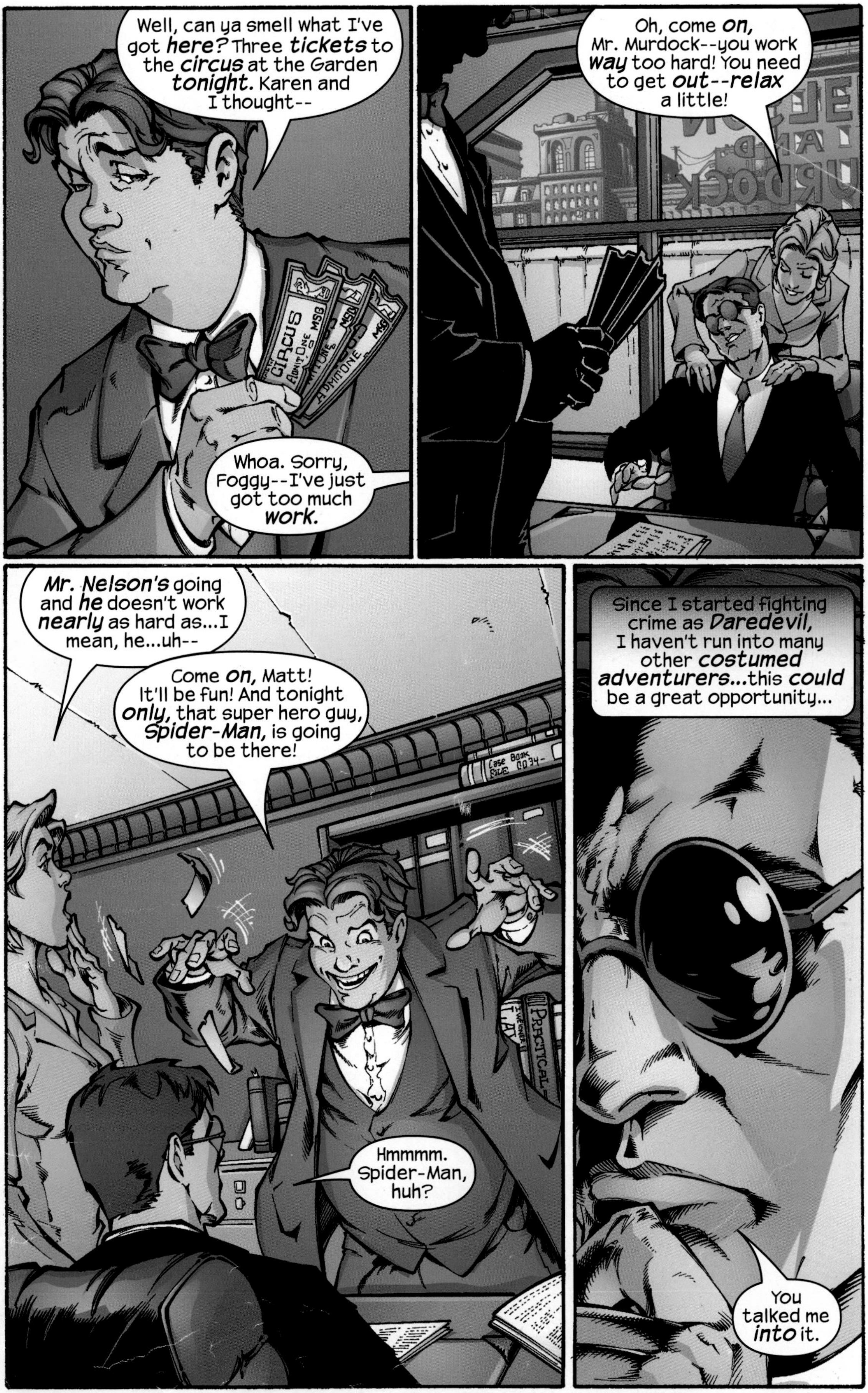
Well, can ya smell what I've got here? Three tickets to the circus at the Garden tonight. Karen and I thought--
CIRCUS ADMIT ONE MSG
ADMIT ONE MSG
MSG
Whoa. Sorry, Foggy--I've just got too much work.
Oh, come on, Mr. Murdock--you work way too hard! You need to get out--relax a little!
Mr. Nelson's going and he doesn't work nearly as hard as...I mean, he...uh--
Come on, Matt! It'll be fun! And tonight only, that super hero guy, Spider-Man, is going to be there!
Hmmmm. Spider-Man, huh?
Since I started fighting crime as Daredevil, I haven't run into many other costumed adventurers...this could be a great opportunity...
You talked me into it.

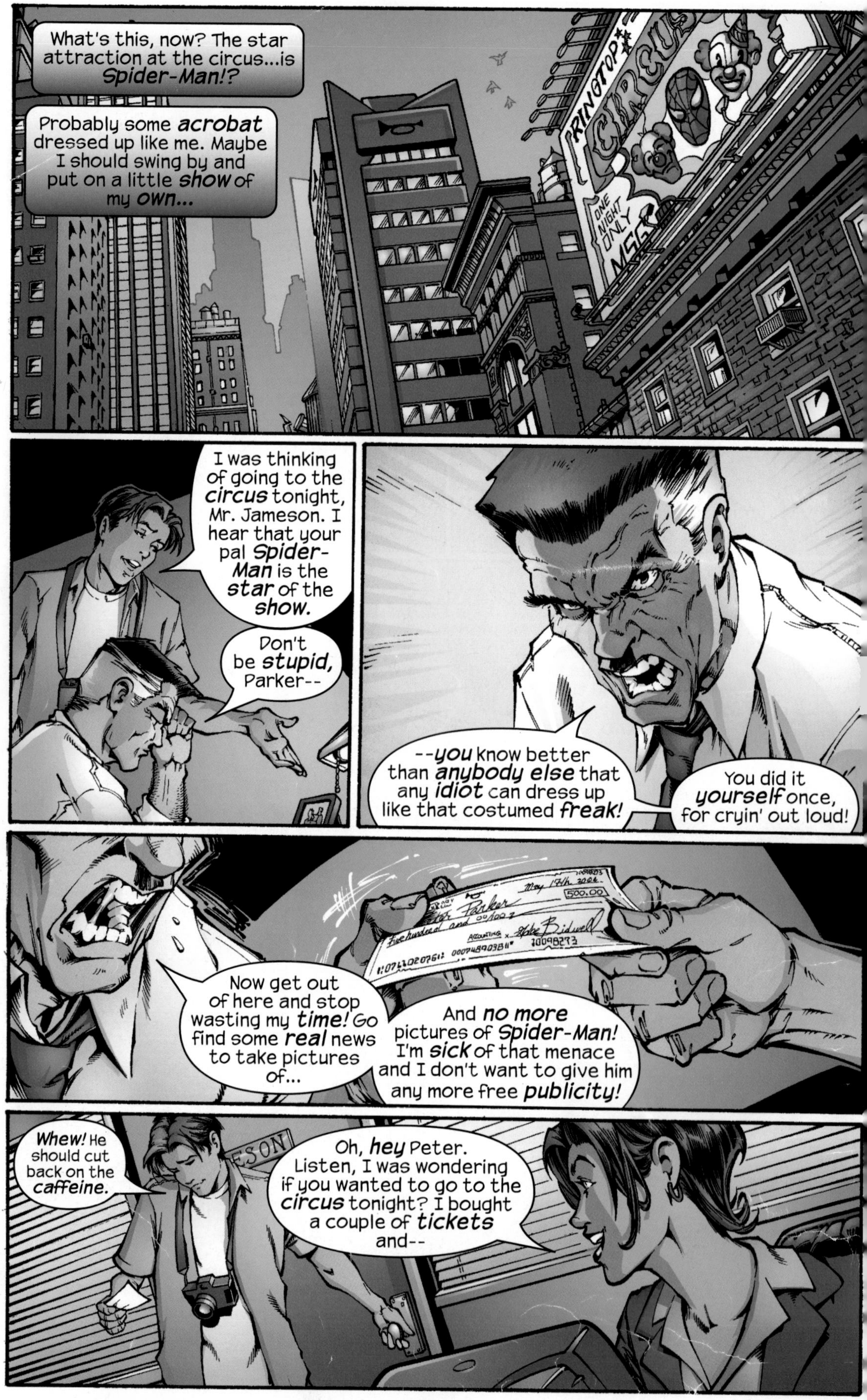
What's this, now? The star attraction at the circus...is Spider-Man!?
Probably some acrobat dressed up like me. Maybe I should swing by and put on a little show of my own...
RINGTOP CIRCUS
ONE NIGHT ONLY MSG
I was thinking of going to the circus tonight, Mr. Jameson. I hear that your pal Spider-Man is the star of the show.
Don't be stupid, Parker--
--you know better than anybody else that any idiot can dress up like that costumed freak!
You did it yourself once, for cryin' out loud!
Now get out of here and stop wasting my time! Go find some real news to take pictures of...
And no more pictures of Spider-Man! I'm sick of that menace and I don't want to give him any more free publicity!
Whew! He should cut back on the caffeine.
Oh, hey Peter. Listen, I was wondering if you wanted to go to the circus tonight? I bought a couple of tickets and--

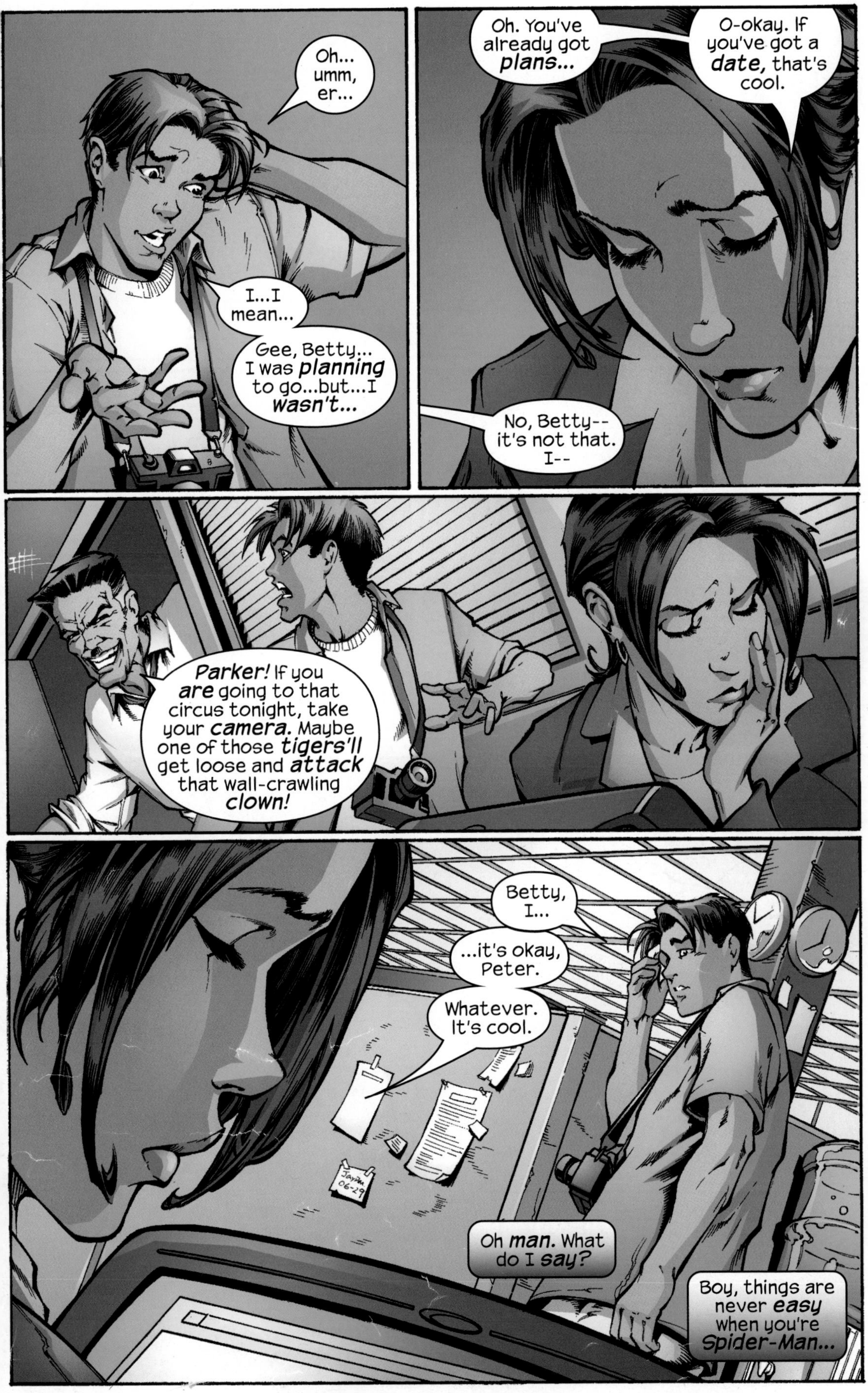
Oh... umm, er...
I...I mean...
Gee, Betty... I was planning to go...but...I wasn't...
Oh. You've already got plans...
O-okay. If you've got a date, that's cool.
No, Betty-- it's not that. I--
Parker! If you are going to that circus tonight, take your camera. Maybe one of those tigers'll get loose and attack that wall-crawling clown!
Betty, I...
...it's okay, Peter.
Whatever. It's cool.
Oh man. What do I say?
Boy, things are never easy when you're Spider-Man...

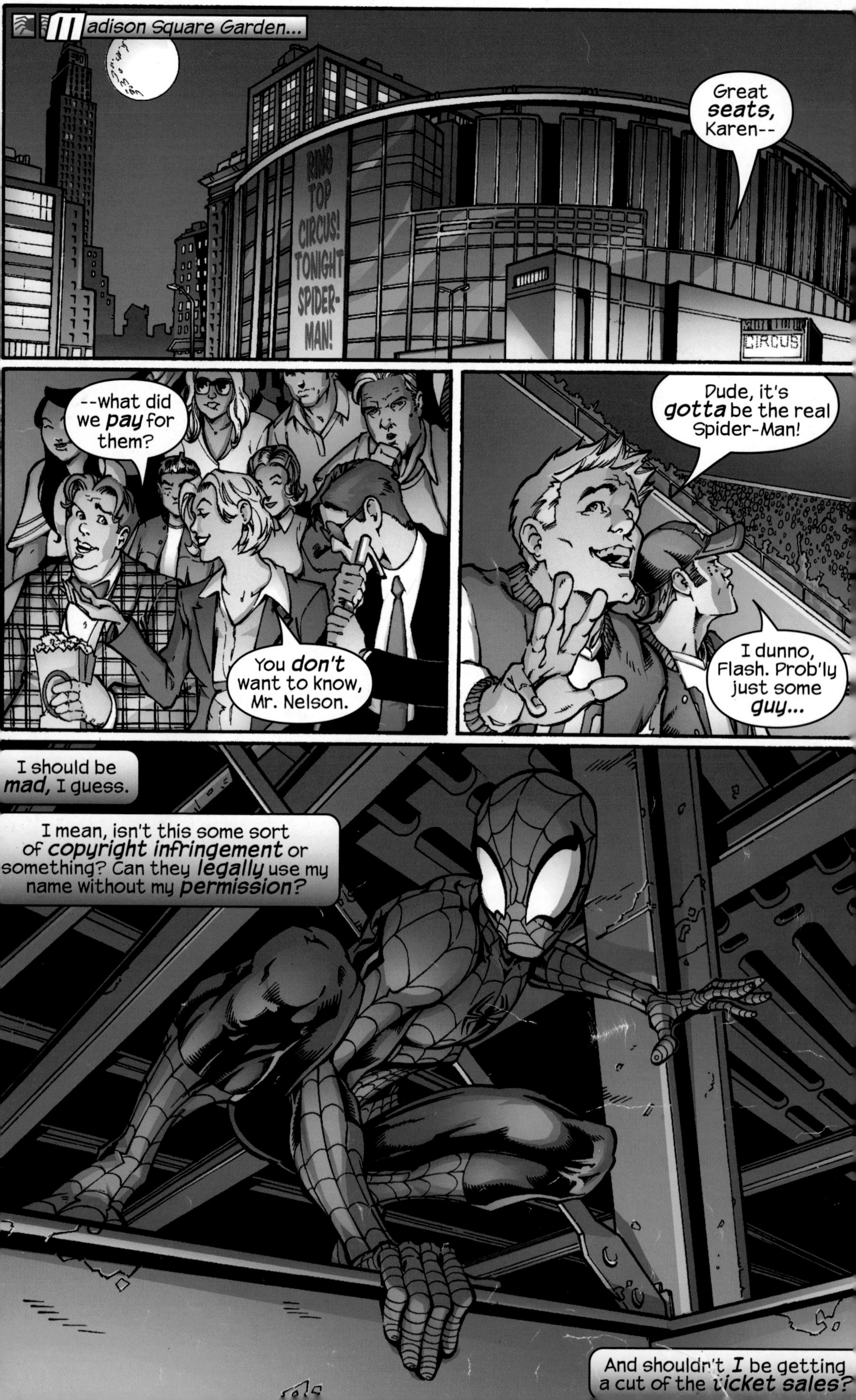

Madison Square Garden...
RING TOP CIRCUS! TONIGHT SPIDER-MAN!
CIRCUS
Great seats, Karen--
--what did we pay for them?
You don't want to know, Mr. Nelson.
Dude, it's gotta be the real Spider-Man!
I dunno, Flash. Prob'ly just some guy...
I should be mad, I guess.
I mean, isn't this some sort of copyright infringement or something? Can they legally use my name without my permission?
And shouldn't I be getting a cut of the ticket sales?

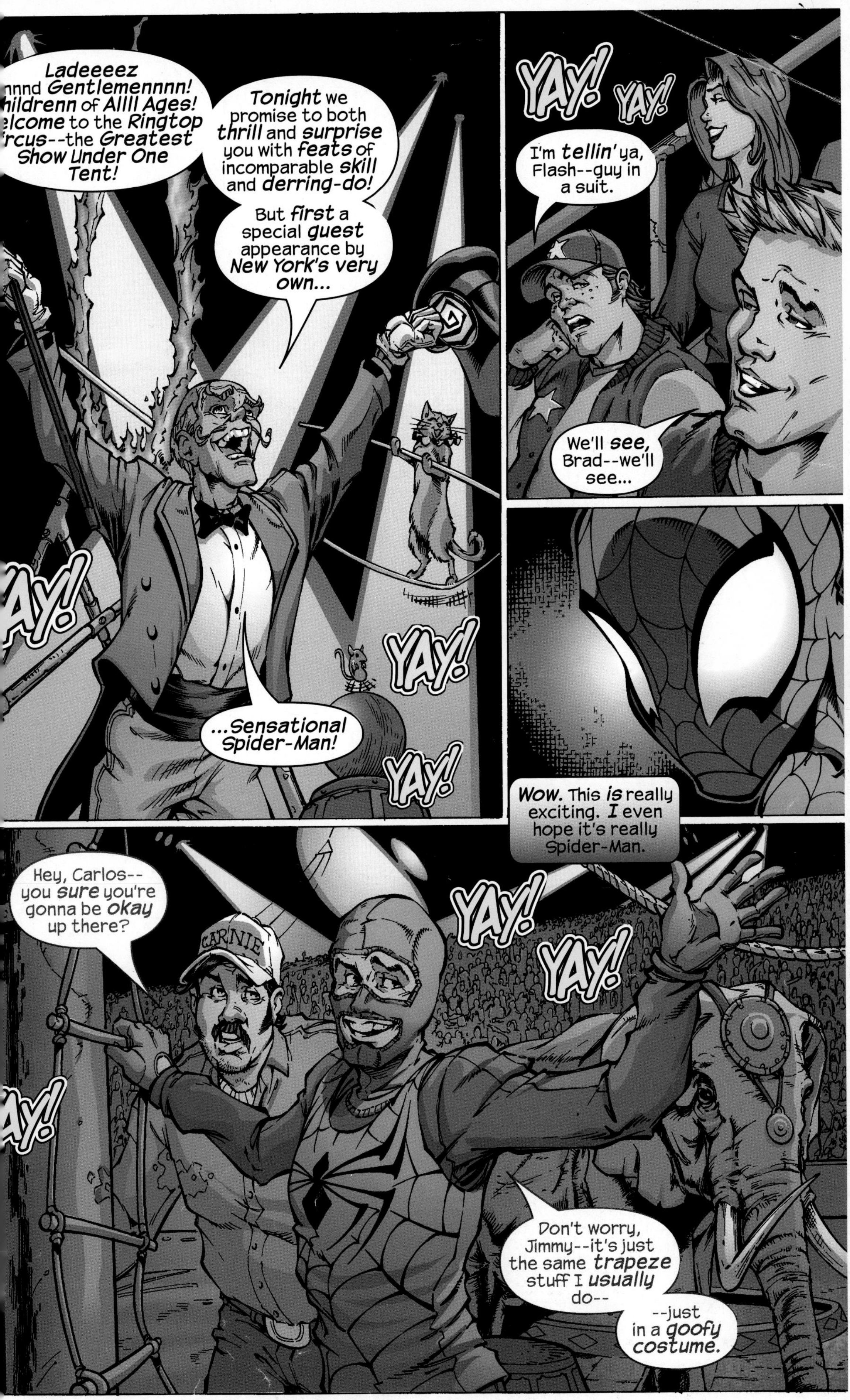

Ladeeeez
nnnd Gentlemennnn!
hildrenn of Allll Ages!
elcome to the Ringtop
ircus--the Greatest
Show Under One
Tent!
Tonight we promise to both thrill and surprise you with feats of incomparable skill and derring-do!
But first a special guest appearance by New York's very own...
...Sensational Spider-Man!
YAY!
YAY!
YAY!
YAY! YAY!
I'm tellin' ya, Flash--guy in a suit.
We'll see, Brad--we'll see...
Wow. This is really exciting. I even hope it's really Spider-Man.
Hey, Carlos--you sure you're gonna be okay up there?
CARNIE
YAY!
YAY!
AY!
Don't worry, Jimmy--it's just the same trapeze stuff I usually do--
--just in a goofy costume.

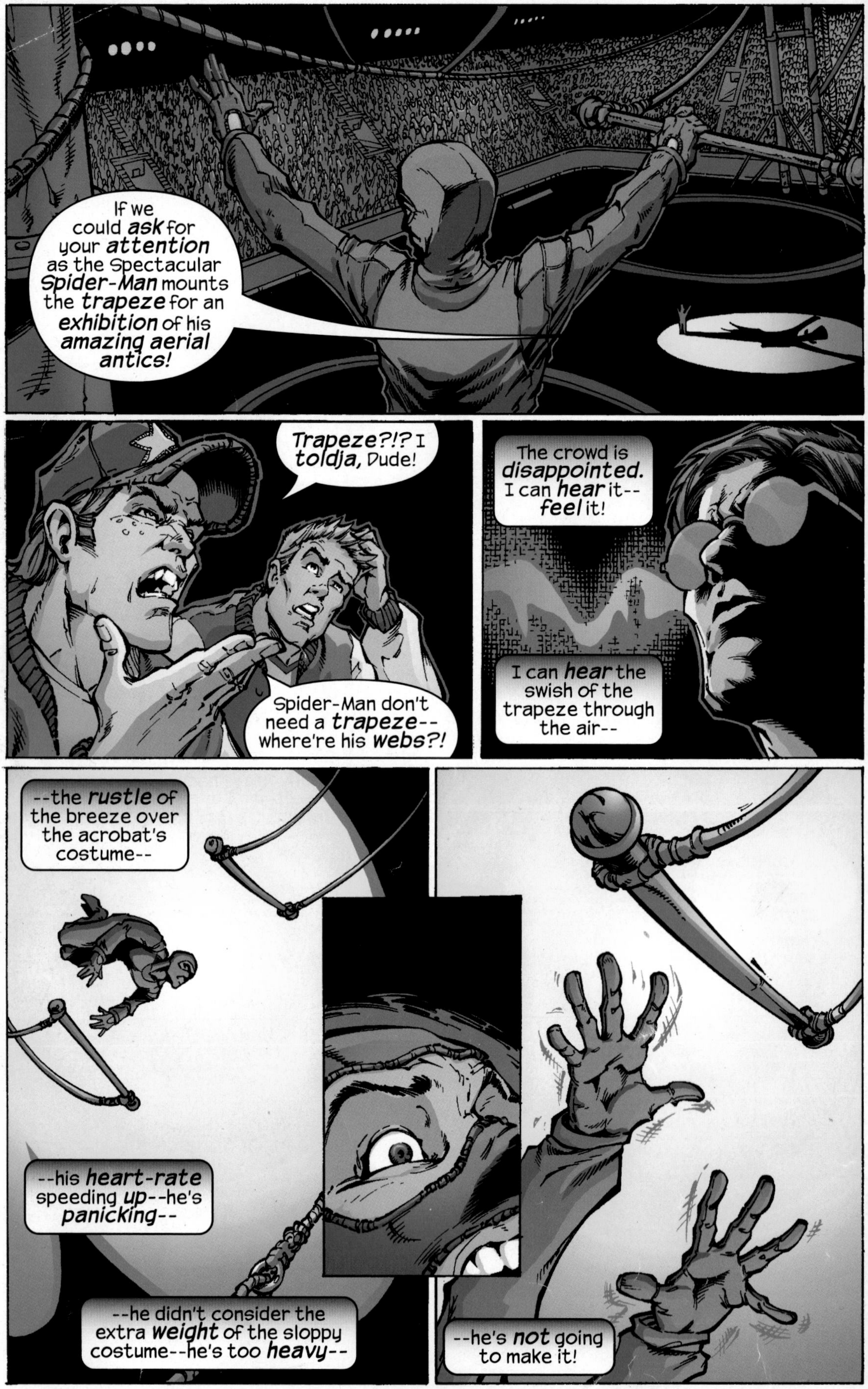

If we could ask for your attention as the Spectacular Spider-Man mounts the trapeze for an exhibition of his amazing aerial antics!
Trapeze?!? I toldja, Dude!
Spider-Man don't need a trapeze--where're his webs?!
The crowd is disappointed. I can hear it--feel it!
I can hear the swish of the trapeze through the air--
--the rustle of the breeze over the acrobat's costume--
--his heart-rate speeding up--he's panicking--
--he didn't consider the extra weight of the sloppy costume--he's too heavy--
--he's not going to make it!

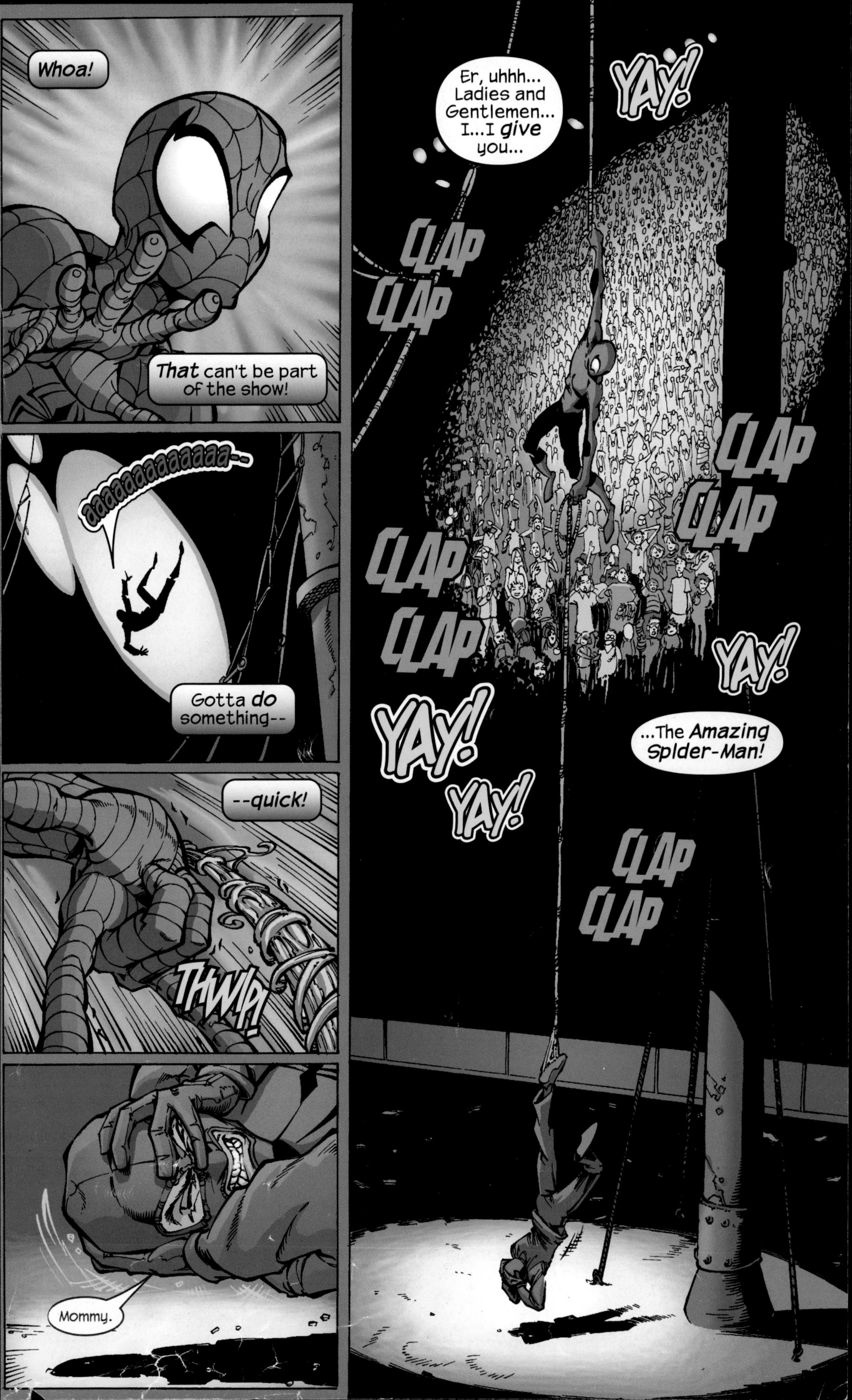
Whoa!
That can't be part of the show!
aaaaaaaaaaaaaa--
Gotta do something--
--quick!
THWIP!
Mommy.
Er, uhhh... Ladies and Gentlemen... I...I give you...
YAY!
CLAP CLAP
CLAP CLAP
CLAP CLAP
YAY!
...The Amazing Spider-Man!
YAY!
YAY!
CLAP CLAP

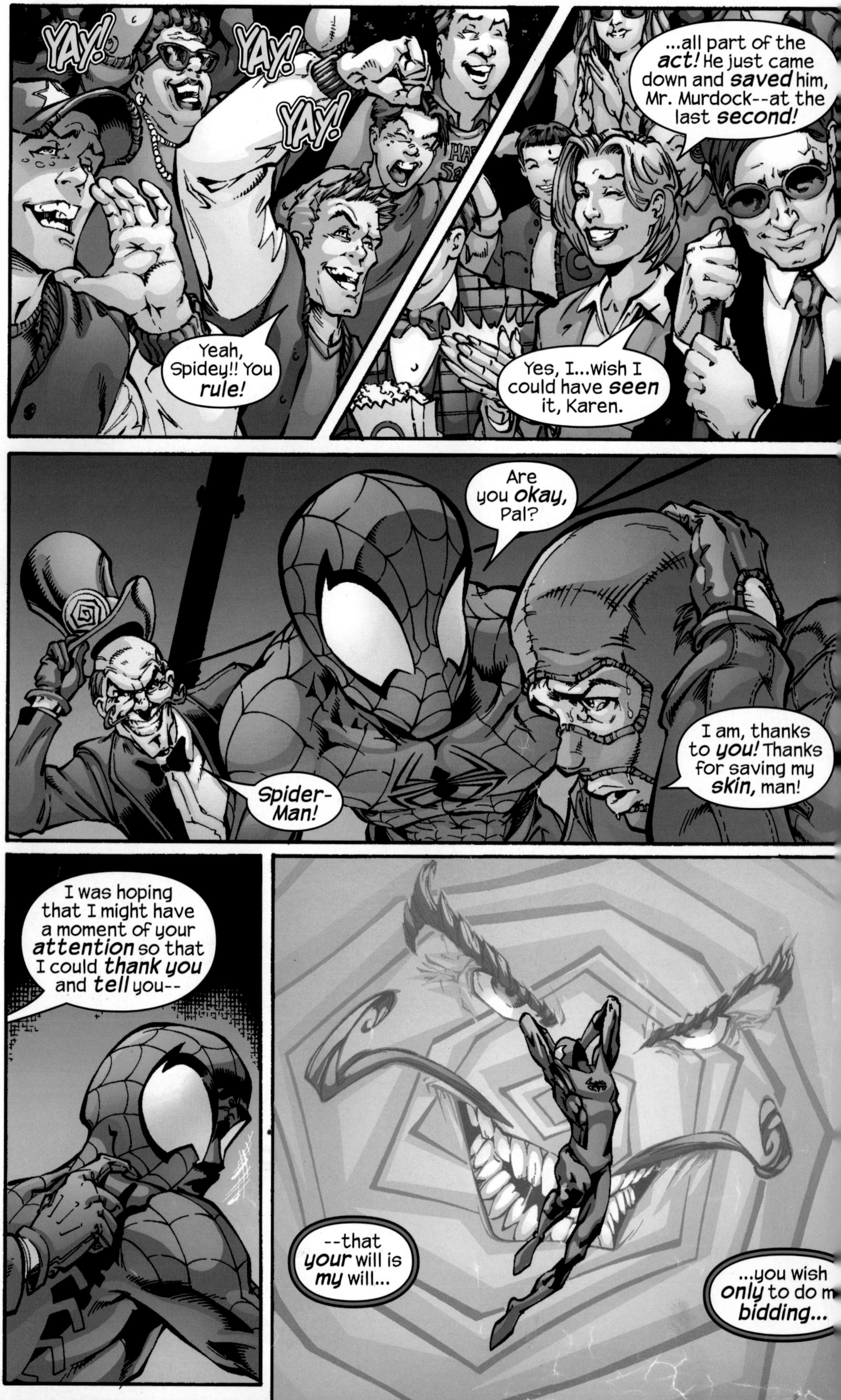
YAY!
YAY!
YAY!
Yeah, Spidey!! You rule!
...all part of the act! He just came down and saved him, Mr. Murdock--at the last second!
Yes, I...wish I could have seen it, Karen.
Are you okay, Pal?
Spider-Man!
I am, thanks to you! Thanks for saving my skin, man!
I was hoping that I might have a moment of your attention so that I could thank you and tell you--
--that your will is my will...
...you wish only to do m bidding...

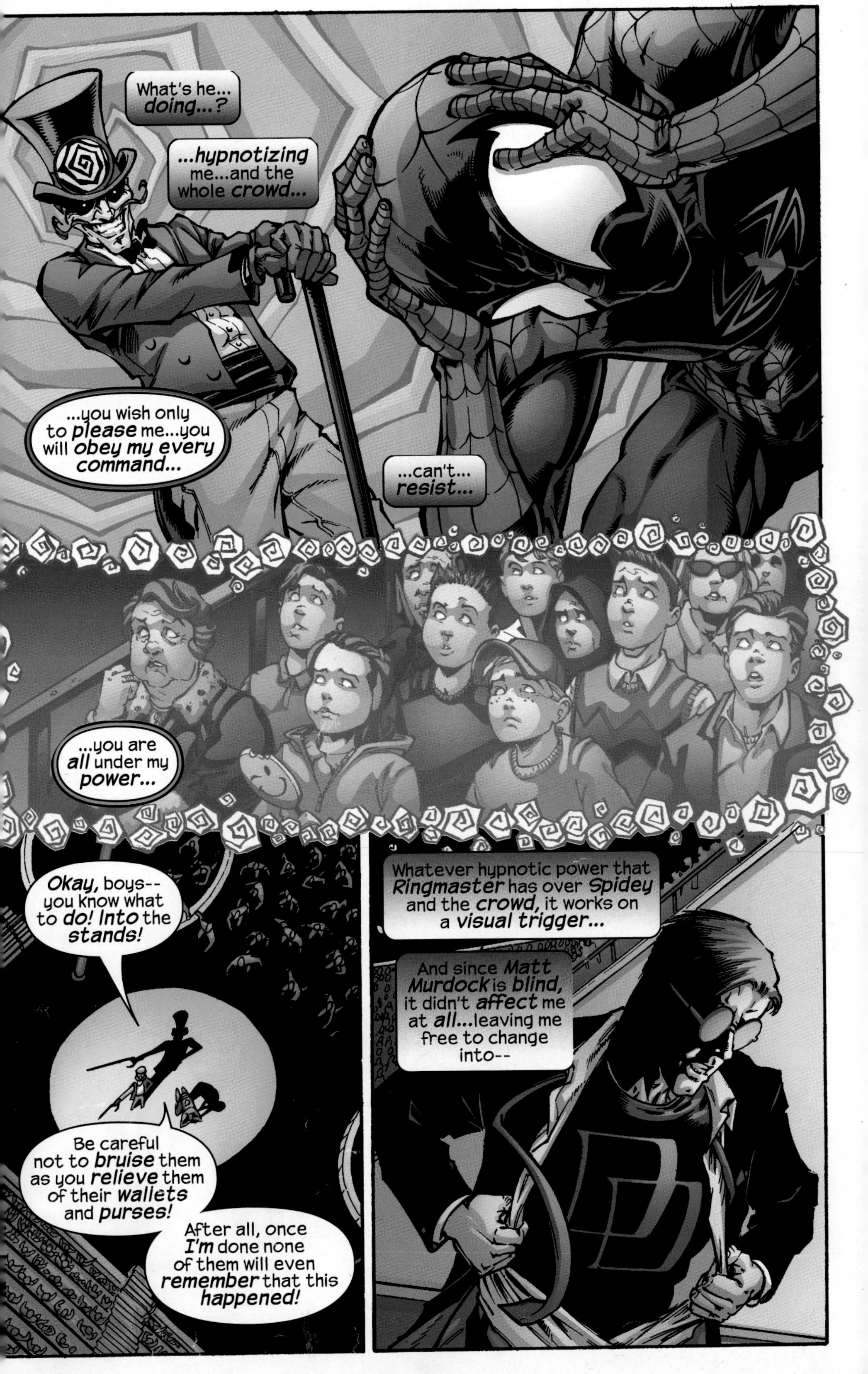
What's he... doing...?
...hypnotizing me...and the whole crowd...
...you wish only to please me...you will obey my every command...
...can't... resist...
...you are all under my power...
Okay, boys-- you know what to do! Into the stands!
Be careful not to bruise them as you relieve them of their wallets and purses!
After all, once I'm done none of them will even remember that this happened!
Whatever hypnotic power that Ringmaster has over Spidey and the crowd, it works on a visual trigger...
And since Matt Murdock is blind, it didn't affect me at all...leaving me free to change into--

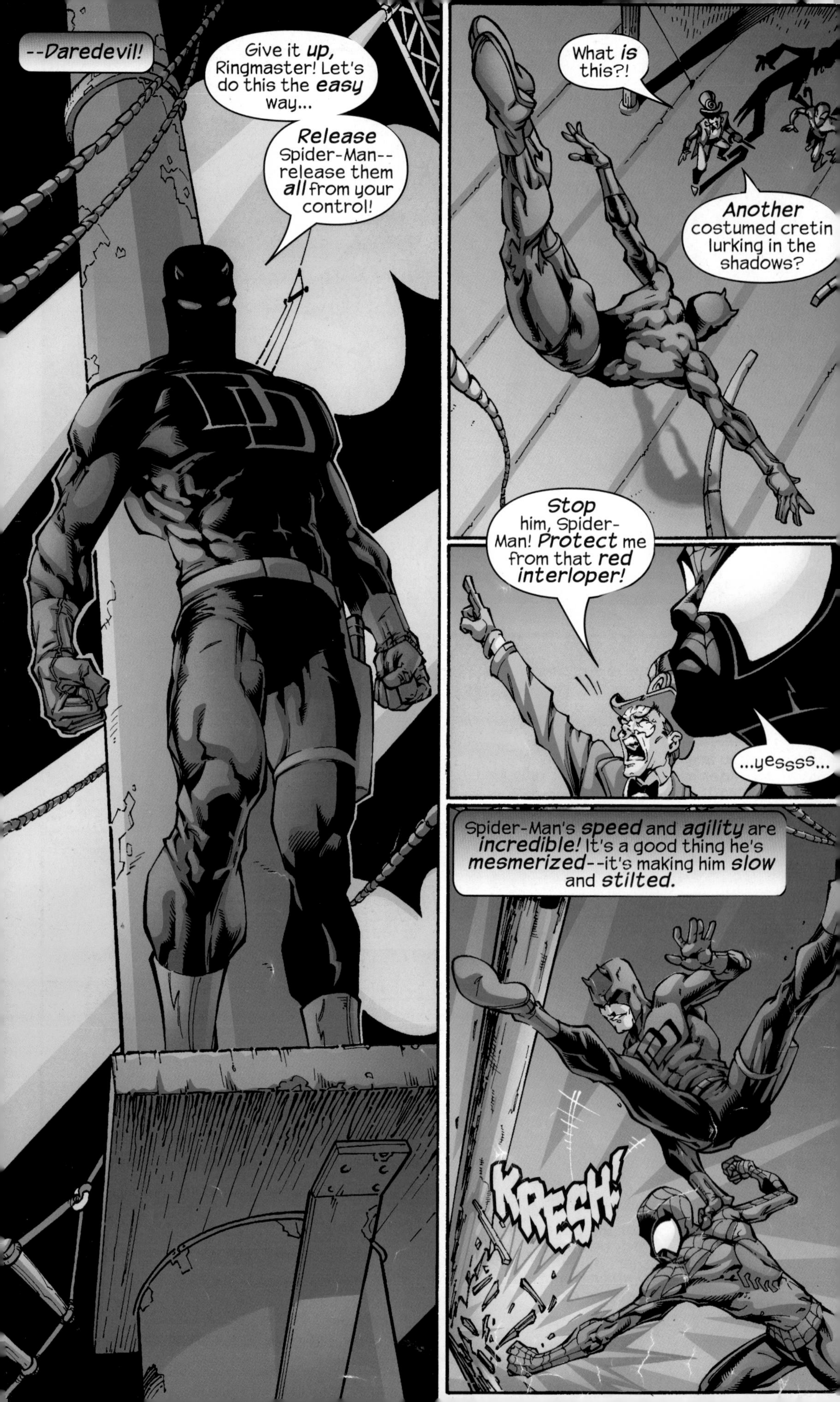
--Daredevil!
Give it up, Ringmaster! Let's do this the easy way...
Release Spider-Man--release them all from your control!
What is this?!
Another costumed cretin lurking in the shadows?
Stop him, Spider-Man! Protect me from that red interloper!
...yessss...
Spider-Man's speed and agility are incredible! It's a good thing he's mesmerized--it's making him slow and stilted.
KRESH!

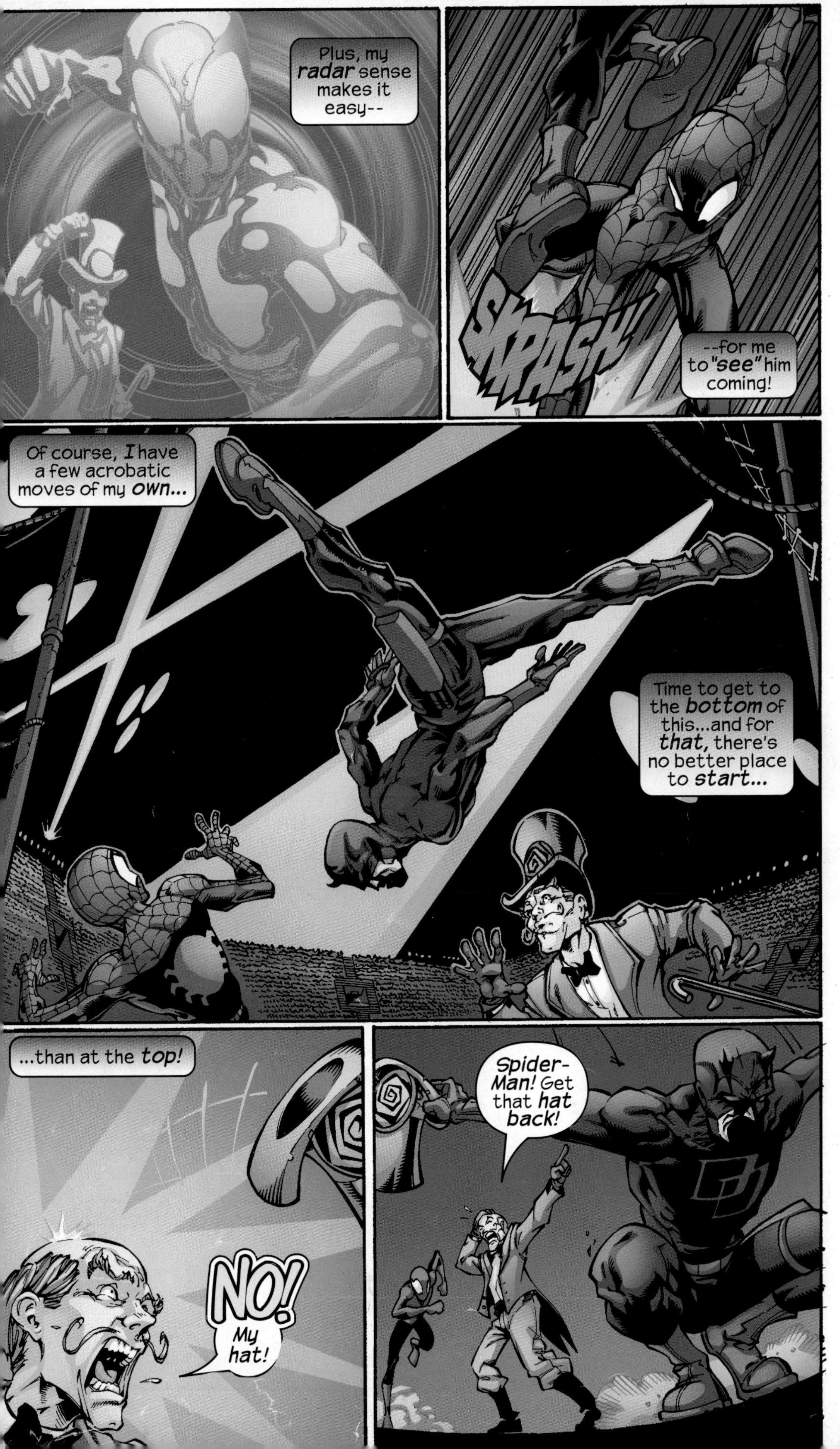
Plus, my radar sense makes it easy--
SKRASH!
--for me to "see" him coming!
Of course, I have a few acrobatic moves of my own...
Time to get to the bottom of this...and for that, there's no better place to start...
...than at the top!
NO! My hat!
Spider-Man! Get that hat back!

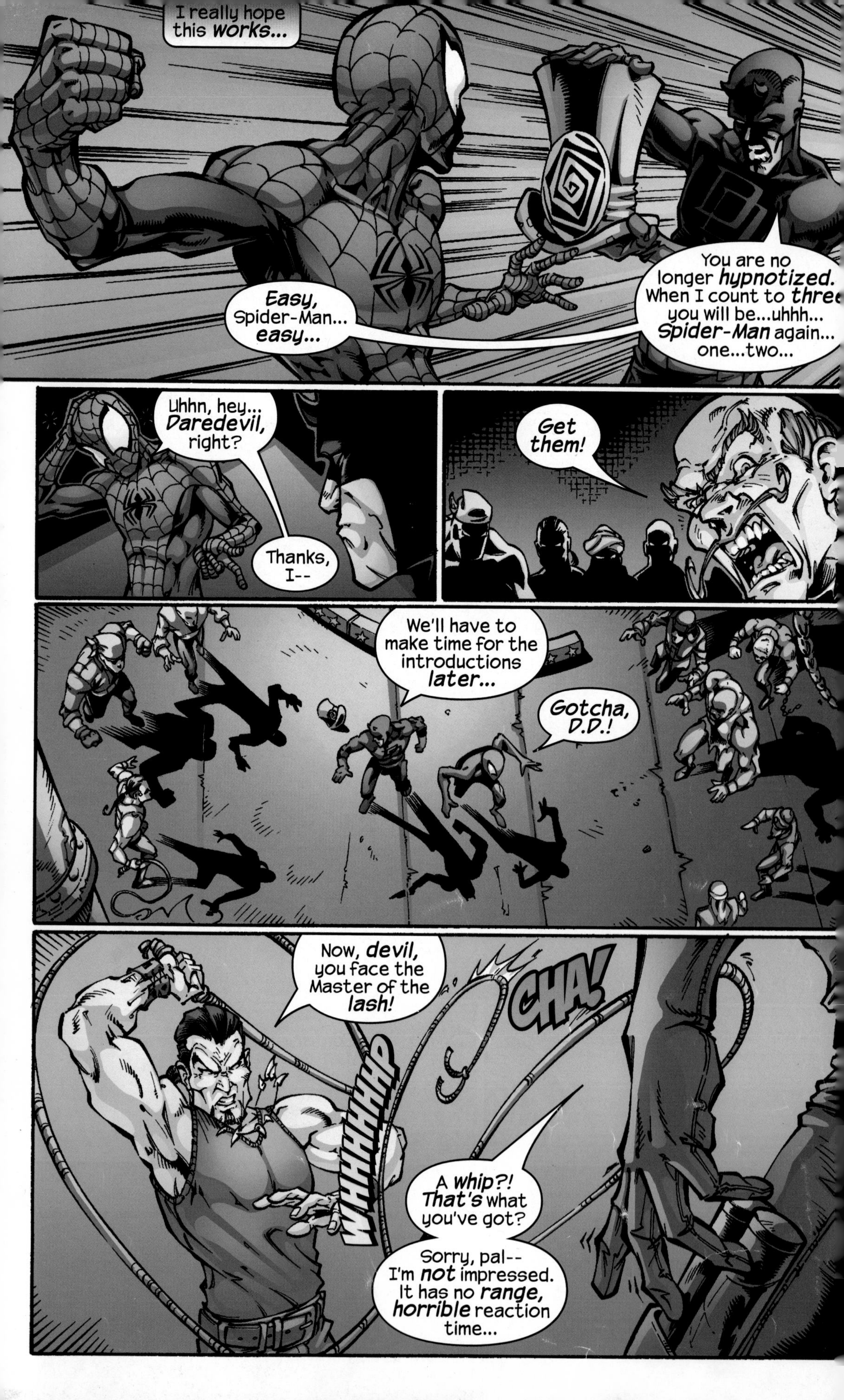
I really hope this works...
Easy, Spider-Man... easy...
You are no longer hypnotized. When I count to three you will be...uhhh... Spider-Man again... one...two...
Uhhn, hey... Daredevil, right?
Thanks, I--
Get them!
We'll have to make time for the introductions later...
Gotcha, D.D.!
Now, devil, you face the Master of the lash!
WHHHHHP
CHA!
A whip?! That's what you've got?
Sorry, pal-- I'm not impressed. It has no range, horrible reaction time...

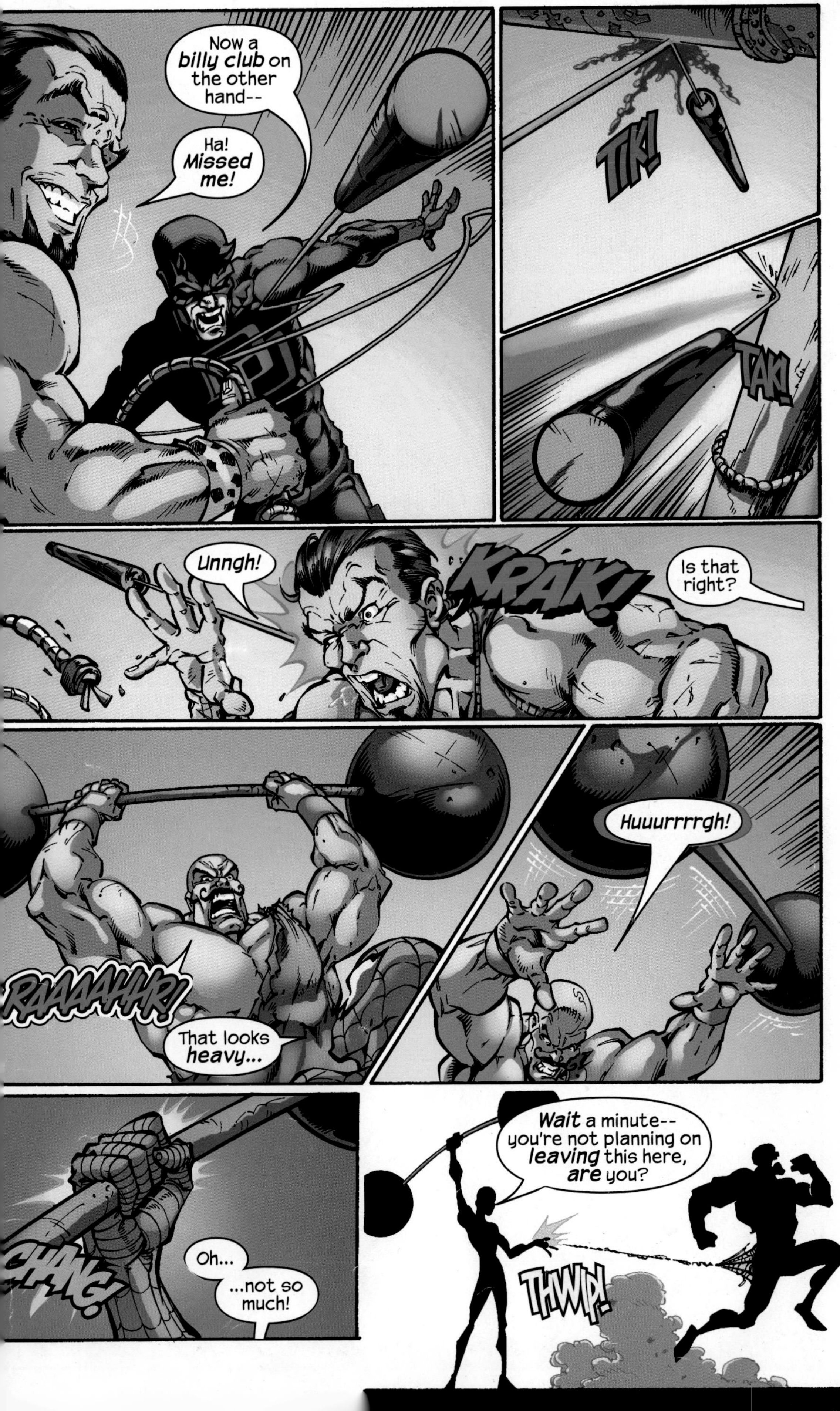

Now a billy club on the other hand--
Ha! Missed me!
TIK!
TAK!
Unngh!
KRAK!
Is that right?
RAAAAHHR!
That looks heavy...
Huuurrrrgh!
CHANG!
Oh...
...not so much!
Wait a minute-- you're not planning on leaving this here, are you?
THWIP!

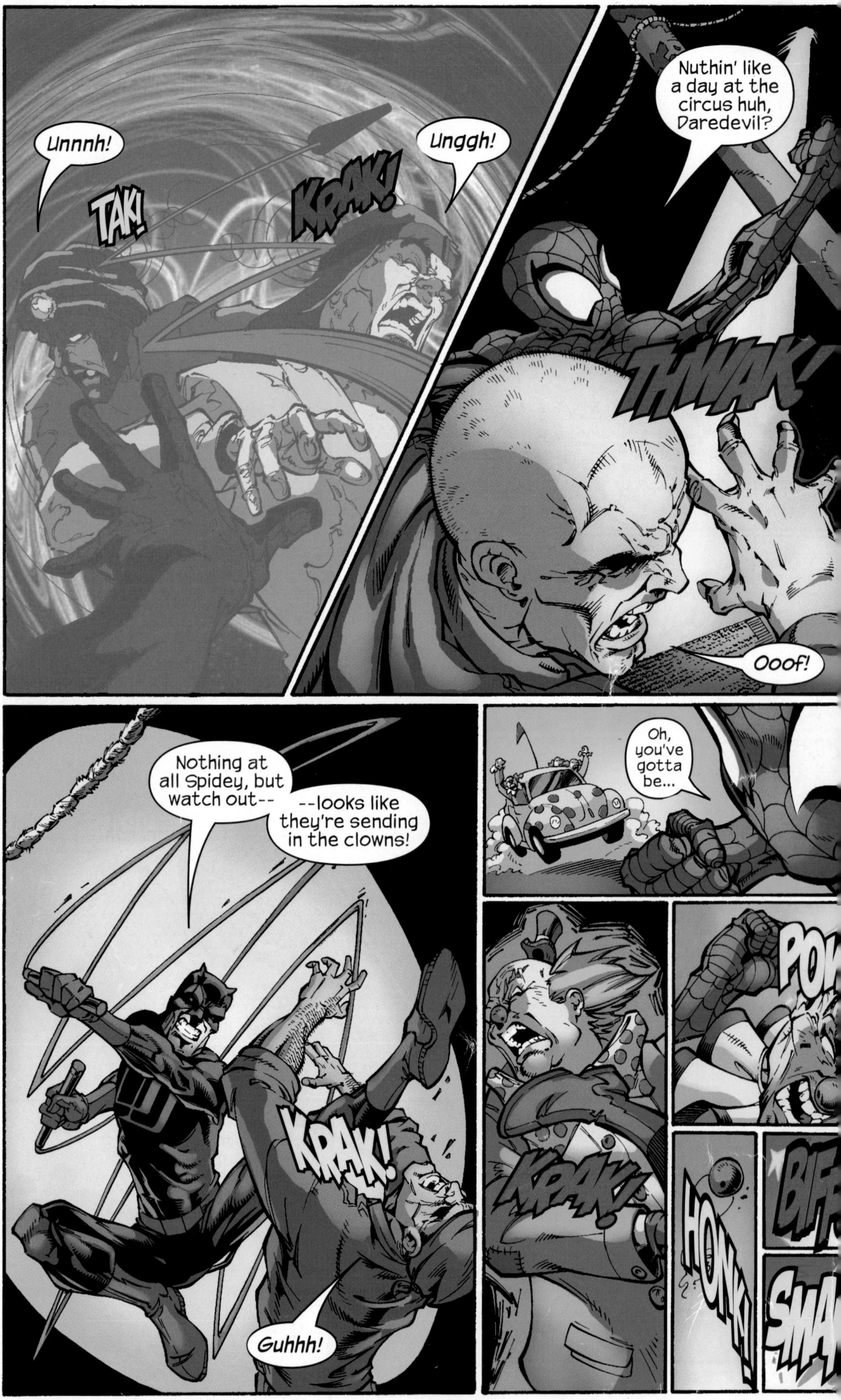

Unnnh!
TAK!
KRAK!
Unggh!
Nuthin' like a day at the circus huh, Daredevil?
THWAK!
Ooof!
Nothing at all Spidey, but watch out--
--looks like they're sending in the clowns!
KRAK!
Guhhh!
Oh, you've gotta be...
KRAK!
HONK!

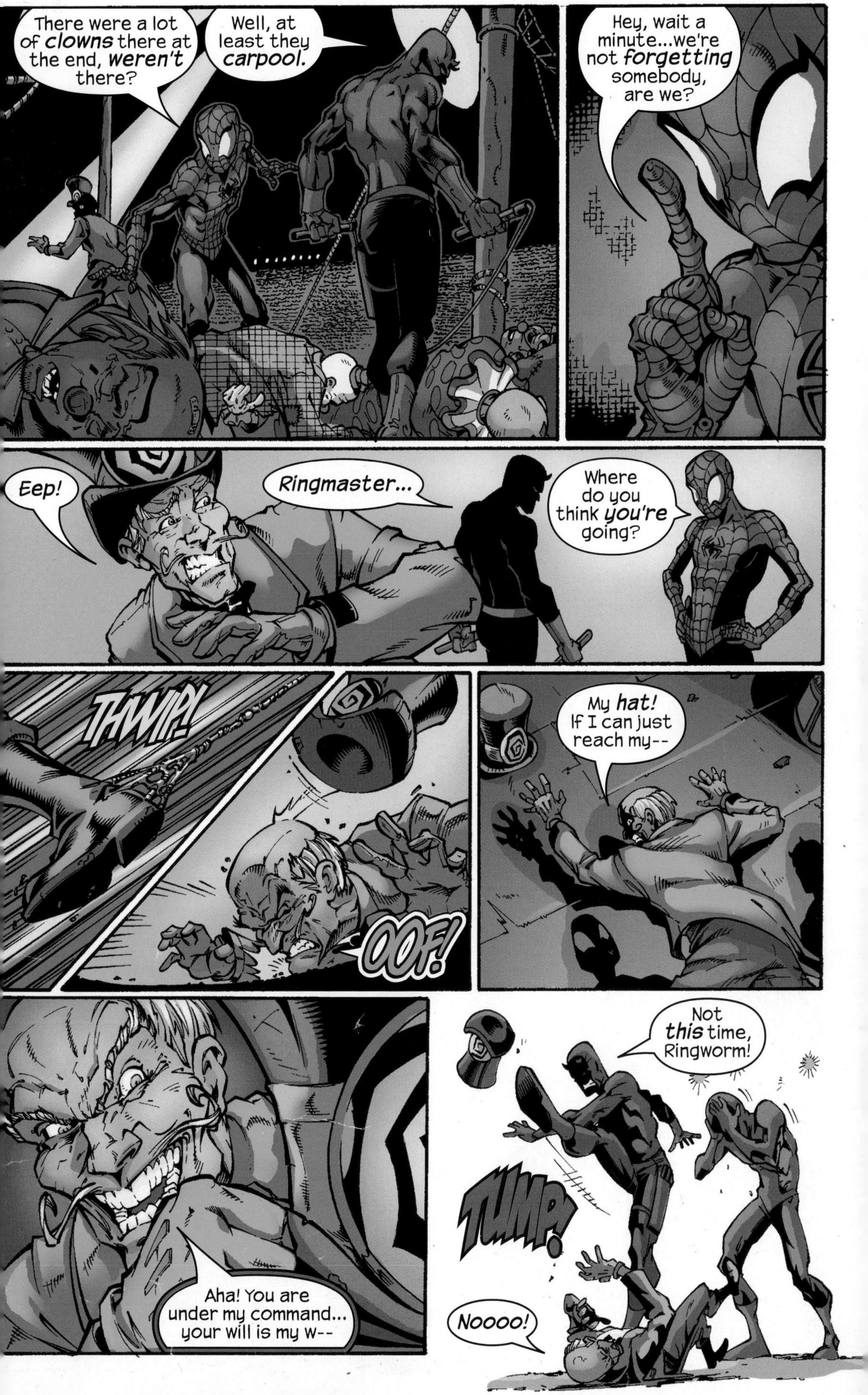

There were a lot of clowns there at the end, weren't there?
Well, at least they carpool.
Hey, wait a minute...we're not forgetting somebody, are we?
Eep!
Ringmaster...
Where do you think you're going?
THWIP!
OOF!
My hat! If I can just reach my--
Aha! You are under my command... your will is my w--
Not this time, Ringworm!
TUMP!
Noooo!

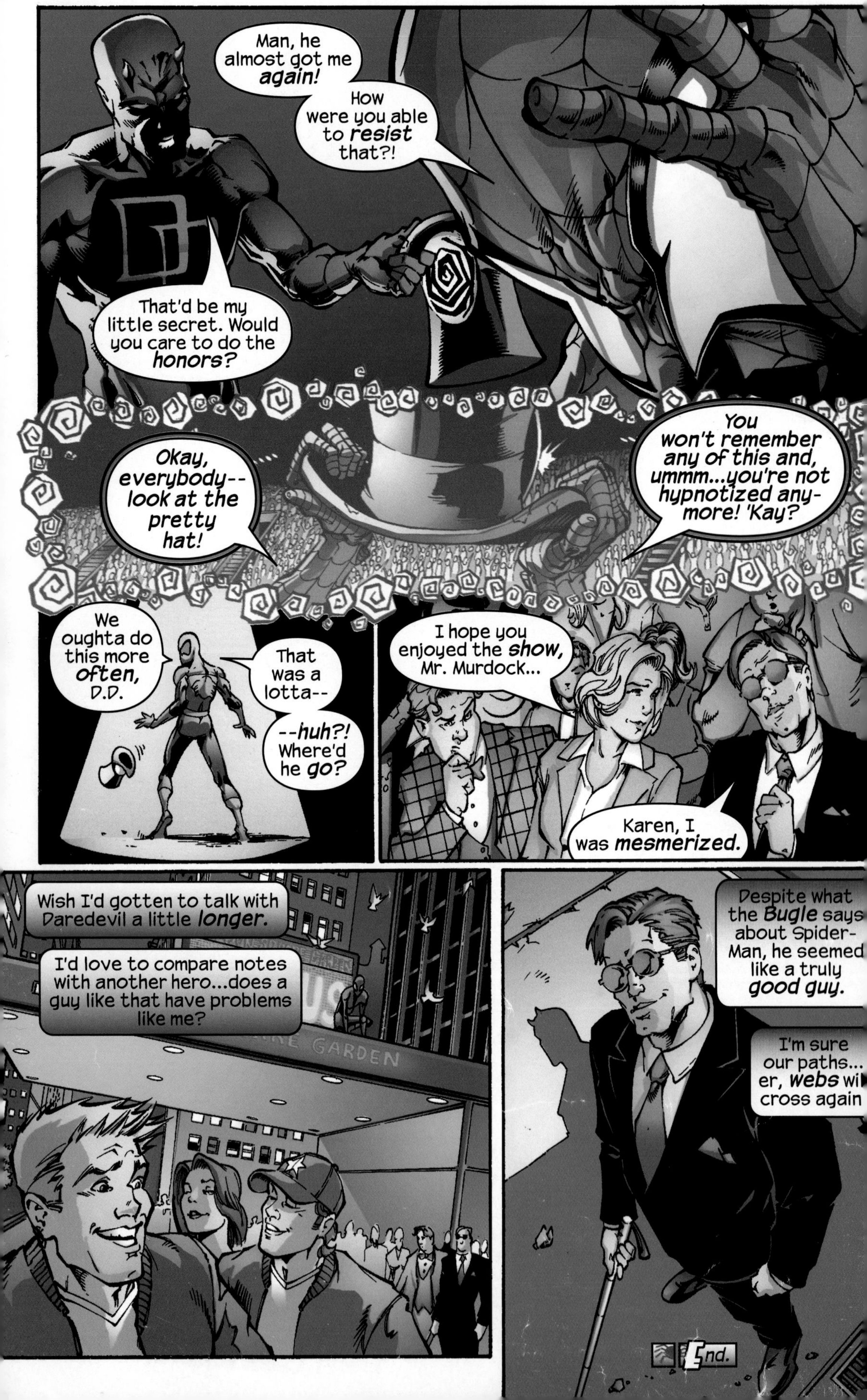

Man, he almost got me again!
How were you able to resist that?!
That'd be my little secret. Would you care to do the honors?
Okay, everybody--look at the pretty hat!
You won't remember any of this and, ummm...you're not hypnotized any-more! 'Kay?
We oughta do this more often, D.D.
That was a lotta--
--huh?! Where'd he go?
I hope you enjoyed the show, Mr. Murdock...
Karen, I was mesmerized.
Wish I'd gotten to talk with Daredevil a little longer.
I'd love to compare notes with another hero...does a guy like that have problems like me?
GARDEN
Despite what the Bugle says about Spider-Man, he seemed like a truly good guy.
I'm sure our paths... er, webs wi cross again
End.